EDGE BOOKS

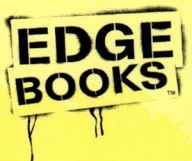

THE WORLD'S TOP TENS

THE WORLD'S FASTEST Animals

by Matt Doeden

Consultant:
Suzanne B. McLaren, Collection Manager
Section of Mammals
Carnegie Museum of Natural History
Edward O'Neil Research Center
Pittsburgh, Pennsylvania

Capstone press
Mankato, Minnesota

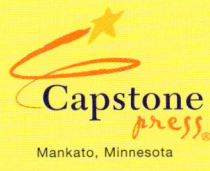

Edge Books are published by Capstone Press,
151 Good Counsel Drive, P.O. Box 669, Mankato, Minnesota 56002.
www.capstonepress.com

Copyright © 2007 by Capstone Press. All rights reserved.
No part of this publication may be reproduced in whole or in part, or stored in a retrieval system, or transmitted in any form or by any means, electronic, mechanical, photocopying, recording, or otherwise, without written permission of the publisher. For information regarding permission, write to Capstone Press, 151 Good Counsel Drive, P.O. Box 669, Dept. R, Mankato, Minnesota 56002.
Printed in the United States of America

Library of Congress Cataloging-in-Publication Data
Doeden, Matt.
    The world's fastest animals / by Matt Doeden.
    p. cm.—(Edge Books. The world's top tens)
    Summary: "Describes 10 of the world's fastest animals in a countdown format"—Provided by publisher.
    Includes bibliographical references and index.
    ISBN-13: 978-0-7368-6436-7 (hardcover)
    ISBN-10: 0-7368-6436-9 (hardcover)
    1. Animals—Juvenile literature. I. Title. II. Edge Books, the world's top tens.
QL49.D62 2007
590—dc22   2006003287

Editorial Credits
Angie Kaelberer, editor; Kate Opseth, set designer; PhaseOne, book designer;
    Wanda Winch, photo researcher; Scott Thoms, photo editor

Photo Credits
Corbis/Galen Rowell, 20, 27 (middle right); Gallo Images/Anthony Bannister, 29;
    Paul A. Souders, 22, 27 (bottom left)
Getty Images Inc./Jamie McDonald, 16; Jonathan Wood, 12, 26 (bottom right);
    Stone/S. Purdy Matthews, 8, 26 (top right)
Minden Pictures/Mitsuaki Iwago, 4
Peter Arnold/Martin Harvey, cover; X. Eichaker, 24
SeaPics.com/Doug Perrine, 18, 27 (middle left); Ingrid Visser, 10, 26 (bottom left)
Shutterstock/Alexander M. Omelko, 6, 26 (top left); Cindy Haggerty, 25,
    27 (bottom right); Konstantine Kikvidze, 7; Winthrop Brookhouse,
    17, 27 (top right)
SuperStock/age fotostock, 14, 15, 27 (top left)

1 2 3 4 5 6 11 10 09 08 07 06

Table of Contents

Fast Animals 4
Number 10 6
Number 9 8
Number 8 10
Number 7 12
Number 6 14
Number 5 16
Number 4 18
Number 3 20
Number 2 22
Number 1 24
Understanding Fast Animals 28

Glossary 30
Read More 31
Internet Sites 31
Index 32

Fast Animals

The red kangaroo hops across the plains of Australia at 30 miles (48 kilometers) per hour. But even that speed isn't fast enough to make our top 10 list.

Nature produces countless adaptations for its creatures. A turtle's hard shell, a caterpillar's camouflage coloring, and a cobra's venomous bite all help these animals survive in a harsh world.

Predator and prey alike share one of nature's most spectacular adaptations—pure speed. In a constant struggle for survival, the ability to chase or flee at high speeds can be a matter of life and death.

In the following pages, we'll look at 10 of the world's fastest animals—on land, in the air, and in the ocean. We'll see how each animal uses the speed nature has provided to survive.

10

Hundreds of millions of years ago, giant dragonflies with wingspans of 2.5 feet (76 centimeters) ruled the skies. Nature's design for this fascinating insect holds true today, although on a much smaller scale.

The dragonfly's two sets of wings move independently of each other.

Dragonfly

FLYING SPEED: 25 to 30 miles (40 to 48 kilometers) per hour
SCIENTIFIC NAME: Anisoptera (suborder)
RANGE: Every continent except Antarctica

Today's dragonflies are a fraction of the size of their ancestors, but they are still the insect world's fastest flier.

Dragonflies may be the perfect hunters of the insect world. Unlike other insects, their two sets of wings are controlled separately. This feature gives them unique maneuverability and speed. No other winged insect can approach their top speed of 25 to 30 miles (40 to 48 kilometers) per hour.

Almost any small insect can serve as dragonfly prey. Their most common meals are mosquitoes, flies, gnats, and ants. They often hunt in the evening, when flying insects are most active.

These ancient hunters can be beautiful and fun to watch—as long as you're not a mosquito.

9

Female lions use their amazing sprinting speed to hunt food for their pride.

Lion

It's no wonder the lion is known as the king of beasts. On the grassy plains of Africa, every animal knows to avoid nature's most magnificent hunter. Sprinting at speeds of 30 to 36 miles (48 to 58 kilometers) per hour, the lion is second in speed only to the cheetah among the big cats.

Teamwork is another reason lions are successful hunters. They live in groups called prides. Female lions in a pride hunt together, using teamwork to corner, flush, and kill prey. The lion's most common victims are zebras and wildebeests, but every animal within range gives it the respect it deserves.

Top speed: 36 miles (58 kilometers) per hour, but only for short distances

Scientific name: *Panthera leo*

Range: Africa and India

8

Swift and deadly, the orca, or killer whale, certainly earns its fearsome name. Working together, a group of orcas can hunt down and attack almost any animal in the ocean.

When orcas breach, they raise their bodies almost completely out of the water.

Orca

Although the orca is called a killer whale, it actually is a member of the dolphin family. Its speed and intelligence make it the ocean's ideal hunter. Its powerful, sleek body propels it to speeds of almost 30 miles (48 kilometers) per hour. Orcas also work in teams to trap and kill their victims, making them even deadlier.

Orcas live mainly in cool coastal waters, where prey is abundant. They hunt fish, seals, sea lions, and even whales and dolphins. They seem to have no interest in eating people, though. Scientists aren't sure why they don't go after swimmers, scuba divers, and surfers. Maybe we just don't taste very good.

Swimming speed: 30 miles (48 kilometers) per hour
Scientific name: *Orcinus orca*
Range: All the oceans of the world, especially cold water

7

Greyhounds wear muzzles to prevent bites during close races.

RUNNING SPEED: 40 miles (64 kilometers) per hour

AVERAGE LIFE SPAN: 10 to 14 years

FYI: Greyhounds are the oldest pure dog breed.

Greyhound

Many dogs run fast, but the greyhound leaves them all in the dust.

Probably first bred in Egypt thousands of years ago, the sleek, speedy greyhound was used as a hunting dog. Today, their main roles are as racing dogs and family pets.

Greyhounds show off their speed at racetracks. The dogs chase a mechanical rabbit around an oval track at speeds of more than 40 miles (64 kilometers) per hour.

Most greyhounds retire from racing by age 3 or 4. People adopt the lucky ones. Greyhounds are calm, affectionate dogs that get along well with children and other pets. But sadly, many more greyhounds are destroyed when their racing days end. It's a cruel fate for man's best—and fastest—friend.

6

The ostrich is probably the world's strangest bird. These huge birds can't fly. Instead, they run. At speeds of more than 45 miles (72 kilometers) per hour, they're easily the fastest of all two-legged animals.

Ostriches are native to Africa, but they also do well in other parts of the world. These birds live on a farm in the Negev Desert of Israel.

Ostrich

Running speed: 45 miles (72 kilometers) per hour
Scientific name: *Struthio camelus*
Range: Central and southern Africa
FYI: The ostrich is the only bird with two toes. Most have four.

The ostrich uses both speed and endurance to run from predators.

The best human athletes run about 27 miles (43 kilometers) per hour, and only for short distances. By contrast, ostriches can keep up a pace of about 30 miles (48 kilometers) per hour for long distances.

Speed and size are important defenses for these birds, which are hunted by cheetahs, lions, and people. At up to 8 feet (2.4 meters) tall, they have a great view of their surroundings. When threatened, they either run or fight with their beaks and powerful legs. If you ever meet one on the plains, you'd better hope it decides to run.

5

Whether it's a mustang galloping across a plain or a Thoroughbred thundering down a racetrack, the horse is built for speed.

Horses gallop over grass courses at Newmarket Racecourse in England. The track is one of the oldest in the world.

Horse

Running speed: 43 miles (70 kilometers) per hour
Scientific name: *Equus* (genus)
Average life span: 20 to 30 years

Wild horses are called mustangs.

The horse's top speed of 43 miles (69 kilometers) per hour doesn't compete with some of the other animals on our list. But horses have something many other animals don't—endurance. Even carrying heavy loads, a horse can keep up a gallop for miles and miles.

Horses were domesticated about 6,000 years ago, but herds of wild horses still roam the plains of Asia and the United States. Whether domesticated or wild, all horses have one thing in common—they're born to run.

4

Few sights in nature are as spectacular as that of a 200-pound (91-kilogram) sailfish leaping out of the water at top speed.

Long, pointed bills and tall dorsal fins make sailfish easy to recognize.

Sailfish

The fastest of all marine animals, sailfish can swim faster than 50 miles (80 kilometers) per hour. They can also leap into the air with powerful bursts of up to 68 miles (109 kilometers) per hour. A leaping sailfish is easy to spot by its long, tall dorsal fin, which looks like a sail.

While these fish aren't good to eat, they are a prized catch by any saltwater fisher. Most sailfish that are caught are briefly admired, then released back into the water. That way, more people can enjoy their speed and grace.

Leaping speed:	68 miles (110 kilometers) per hour
Weight:	128 pounds (58 kilograms) to 220 pounds (100 kilograms)
Scientific name:	*Istiophorus platypterus*
Range:	Mild and warm ocean waters

3

Pronghorn herds scamper over the rocky land of northern Yellowstone National Park in Montana.

Running speed: 60 miles (97 kilometers) per hour
Scientific name: *Antilocapra americana*
Range: Western North America

Pronghorn

North America's fastest land animal is an antelope that's not really an antelope. Despite the pronghorn antelope's name, the animal isn't closely related to the antelopes of Africa. But it does share one thing in common with its African namesake—speed.

Native only to western North America, the pronghorn gets its name from a forward spike, called a prong, on each horn. They live mainly in open, grassy areas and deserts. They graze on grasses, shrubs, cacti, and other plants.

The pronghorn runs at a speed of 60 miles (97 kilometers) per hour. It uses this great speed to escape its predators, which include mountain lions, coyotes, and bobcats. Pronghorns also have great endurance. They can run 30 miles (48 kilometers) per hour for 5 miles (8 kilometers) or farther. These animals have truly earned their nickname—the rocket of the American West.

2

The speedy cheetah usually hunts during the day.

Speed: 65 miles (105 kilometers) per hour or more over short distances

Scientific name: *Acinonyx jubatus*

Range: Central and southern Africa, with a very small population in Iran

Prey: Gazelles, antelope, impalas, warthogs

Cheetah

The cheetah is built like no other mammal on earth. The big cat's entire body, from its narrow waist to its long legs, comes together for one purpose—incredible speed. Cheetahs don't have the brute killing force of their lion and tiger cousins. Instead, they rely on the element of surprise, chasing down prey with amazing bursts of speed. At a sprint, a cheetah can run as fast as 65 miles (105 kilometers) per hour.

But cheetahs aren't distance runners. If they don't catch their prey quickly, they have to stop and rest.

These amazing cats are endangered. Fewer than 15,000 remain on the planet. If their numbers continue to fall, it may be only a matter of time before they disappear forever.

1

If Mother Nature handed out speeding tickets, the peregrine falcon would be in real trouble. Their amazing dives clock in at 200 miles (322 kilometers) per hour. No other animal even comes close to reaching that speed.

Peregrine falcons reach their amazing speeds as they dive for prey.

Peregrine Falcon

DIVING SPEED: More than 200 miles (322 kilometers) per hour
SCIENTIFIC NAME: *Falco peregrinus*
RANGE: Every continent except Antarctica

Today, the peregrine falcon is no longer endangered in North America.

The peregrine falcon isn't a slowpoke in regular flight either. They soar at 75 miles (121 kilometers) per hour while searching for prey. When they spot prey with their keen eyesight, the show really begins. With blistering speed, the falcons dive down and rip into the prey with their sharp talons.

About 35 years ago, the peregrine falcon was nearly extinct. Pesticides such as DDT caused their eggshells to become thin and break before the chicks were ready to hatch. After the pesticides were banned, falcon populations started to recover. By 1999, the birds were no longer considered endangered.

The World's Fastest Animals

10 Dragonfly

9 Lion

Orca **8**

7 Greyhound

Ostrich

6

Horse

5

Sailfish

4

Pronghorn

3

Cheetah

2

Peregrine Falcon

1

27

Understanding Fast Animals

Almost everyone is fascinated by speed. We can only imagine what it feels like to be a horse or a cheetah sprinting across an open plain at top speed.

Speed is an important adaptation for survival, but it's not always enough. Many of the animals on our list are endangered. All the speed in the world can't help them survive in a world where people take over their habitats.

But people can also help endangered animals. Many organizations save animals and support laws that protect them. These groups give future generations a chance to see and learn from these animals too.

Endangered animals find safety on protected nature preserves.

Glossary

adaptation (ad-ap-TAY-shuhn)—a change a living thing goes through to better fit in with its environment

domesticated (duh-MESS-tuh-kay-tuhd)—bred to live or work with people

endangered (en-DAYN-jurd)—in danger of becoming extinct

habitat (HAB-uh-tat)—the natural place and conditions in which a plant or animal lives

marine (muh-REEN)—living in salt water

predator (PRED-uh-tur)—an animal that hunts other animals for food

prey (PRAY)—an animal hunted by another animal for food

pride (PRIDE)—a group of lions living together

sprint (SPRINT)—a short, fast run

Read More

Eckart, Edana. *Cheetah.* Animals of the World. New York: Children's Press, 2005.

Frisch, Aaron. *Pronghorns.* Northern Trek. North Mankato, Minn.: Smart Apple Media, 2002.

Unwin, Mike. *Peregrine Falcon.* Animals under Threat. Chicago: Heinemann, 2004.

Wilcox, Charlotte. *The Greyhound.* Learning about Dogs. Mankato, Minn.: Capstone Press, 2001.

Internet Sites

FactHound offers a safe, fun way to find Internet sites related to this book. All of the sites on FactHound have been researched by our staff.

Here's how:

1. Visit *www.facthound.com*
2. Choose your grade level.
3. Type in this book ID **0736864369** for age-appropriate sites. You may also browse subjects by clicking on letters, or by clicking on pictures and words.
4. Click on the **Fetch It** button.

FactHound will fetch the best sites for you!

31

Index

cheetahs, 9, 15, 22, 23, 28

dragonflies, 6–7

endangered animals, 23, 25, 28
endurance, 15, 17, 21

fins, 19

greyhounds, 12, 13

horses, 16–17, 28
hunting, 7, 9, 10, 11, 13, 15

lions, 8, 9, 15, 23

orcas, 10–11
ostriches, 14–15

peregrine falcons, 24–25
predators, 5, 15, 21
prey, 5, 7, 9, 11, 22, 23, 25
prides, 9
pronghorns, 20, 21

racing, 13, 16

sailfish, 18–19
sprinting, 9, 23, 28

wings, 6, 7